WILDEST MOMENTS

frogsnotpigeons

Derek Finn

frogsnotpigeons

Eyes like wildflowers - Only the demons have changed.

CONTENTS

FOREWORD

Humans are by evolution, social animals that tell and listen to stories. This is how we make sense of the world around us and how we communicate with others. We see patterns in cloud formations, interpret meaning in distant star formations and developed advanced intelligence to connect tidal patterns to the gravitational field of the moon. It was the early hunter gatherer who learned to predict the pattern of migration of wild animals that survived and passed this genetic trait on to later generations. Mathmatics, music and language are all patterns that our minds can process to generate meaning. So it is with story telling.

In these short stories, the reader is invited to read meaning from each story into their own particular circumstances, to read with an open mind and to let your imagination take you.

We are frogsnotpigeons.

DISTANT SILENCE

'I thought that I heard you in the distance' speaks the Witch softly. Her eyes look up to see the shadow of the Switchman.

'You have brought much suffering and hardship to many lands' she continues, 'but you are not the first and will also pass.'

'Perhaps you are right' responds the Switchman in a deep tone.

'Ah…. and a face mask to welcome me' he smirks.

The Witch does not respond but instead adjusts her facemask nervously as the Switchman steps forward from the shadows.

'You know, I have been surprised many times by your kind, and this time is no different.'

'I'm not sure what you mean. Tell me what has surprised you?' speaks the Witch.

The Switchman does not respond as though dismissive of her question and instead circles the Witch slowly, as though a sparrow-hawk circling in the sky teasing with its potential prey in the long grass.

'We are not so different Witch' he says in a low voice.

The Witch stands in the centre and feels the Switchman circling, drawing nearer. His presence brings fear and despair to many.

'Remove the mask that I can see your face clearer' he whispers to the Witch over and over as his shadow closes in.

'I don't think so' she retorts, 'there is nothing here for you today'.

With that, the shadow cast by the Switchman starts to recede. The Witch feels the dark start to lift. Looking to the sky the

Witch sees sunlight coming through the trees and birds fill the sky as though to welcome a new day. She thinks to herself how easy it is to forget what is important and knows that the Switch-man will return soon vowing to be ready for the next visit. And so, the story begins. A story told in a climate of World Pandemic, lockdowns, social distancing, and isolation.

When rainbows became a symbol of hope and wearing of face masks became a news media story debated hourly.

SNAP REVENGE

After a couple of weeks of lockdown and social distancing, the Witch is musing what box set she will watch next. Reaching for the TV remote, her hand instead finds a mobile phone that is not hers. Finding it unlocked, the Witch decides to scroll through the messages. After all, if it is not hers, then it must belong to Robert, she muses.

A single name appears more often than others with prolific messaging in FrogSnap. Doreen, the young bookstore lady, is prominent in the texts and the conversations and pics are not about literary works down the library either.

As the Witch reads the messages her eyes fill with tears realising that her own texts and shared selfies are not in the phone as though Robert has deleted her and their shared experiences. Betrayal is the dominant feeling of this Witch and a sadness in her heart. Her Pigeon friend on the Kitchen table looks on as though sharing the Witch's sadness. The Witch continues to flick through pages revealing a developing story line of past encounters of two people sharing to Instagram and FrogSnap. In that moment, the Witch forgets reality and allows her mind to create a soap opera that influences her thoughts.

'I knew that man was not to be trusted' she mutters back to the Pigeon, her voice starting to break. Starting to tremble and stutter with rising anger.

'I have made a mistake to let him back into my life. It is not the fact that I was with him only last week but the feeling of betrayal that is so hard. All my hopes are with him. I gave him my heart and although it is broken, they will both know that it is still beating' she vows in a vengeful tone.

The Pigeon is staring back at the Witch. As sadness turns, the two are becoming one in anger and plans of retribution are forming. The Witch places her mixing bowl on the table with an assortment of strange ingredients in different jars.

Mixing and pounding the bowl contents, the Witch starts to recite a spell of wolves and teeth with the name of Doreen mentioned repeatedly in a sermon of ancient words. As the spell is cast out of revenge, the room is filled with smoke from burning incense creating shadows and the colliding of different worlds. The Pigeon is holding itself together. Just barely. Cooo.... Cooo....

Just then, the Witch's brother Simple Wizard Naleek enters the room waving hands to clear the smoke aside. He walks purposely towards the table and picks up the mobile phone.

'There it is, I've been looking for my cell phone all morning – my assistant is probably trying to contact me'.

The Witch and the Pigeon realise the mistake together – it is NOT Robert's phone but that of her brother Naleek! Once called, the 'horned hunter' of the night cannot be recalled and is already arriving at the Book Store to visit Doreen.

Be Careful and thoughtful when you speak. Sometimes, words can be forgiven but not forgotten. Revenge taken in haste returns with plenty to sit with those that wait its outcome.

TAKEN BY THE SKY

It is quite late now and a dark night with the wind blowing. The eighth of the season, Storm Hanna is in town.

Arriving late at the Witch's house, Naleek is surprised to find the house in darkness – but the motion sensor lights have never worked properly since installed day one. Entering the front door, he calls out to his sister but there is no response. This is strange he thinks to himself. Except to put the bins out, my sister has not left the house in weeks since the lockdown came into effect.

Through the kitchen window, Naleek catches a glimpse of movement in the garden. Opening the back door, he sees his sister standing in the back-garden arms outstretched.

'Sister, what are you doing out here? Come inside for tea' he shouts. However, the sister does not respond direct to Naleek, she instead shouts to the sky.

'Take me Hanna, take me to the sky'.

'What the crikey doodles are you on about woman – are you talking to the wind now?' shouts Naleek to his sister.

She cries back over the wind, 'Leave me brother, I want to be with the sky. I am by myself for too long now'.

Suddenly, the wind dies down and there is silence. The sister drops her arms to her side as though an invisible weight above her is now gone. The only sound that breaks the silence is the faint, and somewhat distressed, rivet, rivet, rivet noise coming from Naleek's pocket.

Every day we have the opportunity to make a difference. If there is even a slight chance of getting something that makes you happy, then risk it. Life is too short and happiness too rare.

I HAD A DREAM

After the excitement of the storm last week, and the antics of the Witch in the back-garden shouting at the sky, it is quiet now at the witch's house. The Witch is sitting at the kitchen table staring into space.

'What are you thinking sister?' asks the simple Naleek from across the two-meter table.

'What does that matter to you' she scorns back to her brother.

Naleek points to the frog on the table 'I brought your frog to the bookstore and found out that it has already read every book in the store!' he exclaims with hands waving excitedly. 'If it can read then maybe it can keep you company with conversation'.

'What are you talking about, brother? Tell me why you think the frog can read' exclaims the Witch with some irritation in her tone.

Her brother looks at her wisely and explained that each time the Frog was presented with a book at the bookstore it responded repeating the same word over and over 'reddit, reddit, reddit'.

This time the Witch moves her stare to her brother, 'you are a simple man brother, and I know well meaning. Even a broken clock is right twice a day – but I have no company from the frog or the pigeon.'

A tear fills Naleek's eye as an understanding grows across his consciousness.

'Let me tell you this story my sister. I was watching prawns swim playfully in the shallow sea without a care in the world. A shark swam up to them and scattered the prawn friends in different directions. Two of the prawn friends, Justin and Christian, swam so far out that they entered deep water where they met a Cod.

The Cod, surprised to see prawns this far out, asks 'what are you doing out here?'

Justin cries – 'I'm tired of being a small prawn – please turn me into a big shark that I will have no fear of anything'. The Cod grants Justin his wish and turns the prawn Justin into a shark.

With that, his friend Christian scatters in fear.

Months pass and Justin swimming alone is so lonely since no one will play with a shark. He goes in search of the Cod and begs to turn him back into a prawn.

Eventually, the Cod reverses the spell and turns Justin back into the prawn.

Justin rushes round to his old friend Christian's little prawn house. Shouting through the letter box,

'Christian, it's me Justin, come out to play'.

But Christian hides in the back refusing to answer, terrified that he will be eaten by the shark.

Justin shouts through the letter box again' It's me Justin, I met Cod, I'm a prawn again Christian'.

The people who belong in your life will find you and stay.... do not be afraid of being yourself. Be afraid of trying to be someone else to please others

THE CROAK OF A FROG

Once the tears had subsided, there is a silence between the simple wizard Naleek and his sister broken only by the croaking of the frog on the table, sounding weak from dehydration.

Naleek interjects trying to make conversation. 'Have you booked any holidays yet sister?'

There is no response from the witch who has resumed her stare through the window.

'Sister!' Naleek raises his voice to try break the sisters fixed stare.

It works. 'I have no holidays booked' she answers sharply. 'I have no interest in such distractions and never liked the sun beach thing anyway. That was always his interest. Robert was like a greyhound in speedos on the beach'.

'I know that you still miss Robert sister, but surely after all this time it's time to move on – get yourself back on the dating website thing. Maybe use a fake photo this time?' Naleek ventures.

'My brother, your nagging is starting to do my head in now – leave me in peace and never mention that name again 'she cries.

Naleek, the simple, thinks to himself, surely a broken relationship can be fixed as he slips a small plate of water under the nose of the dehydrating frog on the table.

'My sister, if I call Robert on his cell phone to invite him for tea, will you at least talk to him?'. The sister turns slowly towards her brother.

'You will not need to call very loud' she says. Her gaze dropping slowly to the frog on the table…'he is not so far'.

You know, not every game in life will be fair. Play anyway

MICE AT THE CROSSROADS

The following week is quiet at the witch's home. It is not like she gets many visitors anymore since the arrival of the COVID. Time to think to herself as she watches shadows taking shape in the fading sunlight wondering what they might mean. The frog is watching from the kitchen table too. Blinking nervously every now and then as frogs do.

She looks back at the frog wondering to herself how she has come to be alone at this time of her life with a frog and a simple wizard for a brother. Tired of counting mice at the crossroads, sitting at this kitchen table ripping pages from the phone book for fun. With only a dumb ass Frog and a manic Pigeon for company.

All I have ever wanted is a companion, a soul mate to keep me company, a cuddle. 'Please forgive me Robert, I am sorry that I turned you into a frog, it was jealousy and I regret it now. Not sure if we can get back to where we were. But I am willing to try if you are?'

The slightly demented frog licks its own eyeballs, blinks, and stares back at the witch. As you might imagine, he looks slightly fearful on the table as the wild-haired woman cowers over him, eyes transfixed on the poor creature. He does nothing more than slightly lift his shoulders and blinks.

Impatient, the witch asks. 'What do you think frog, could we try again?'.

A flapping noise outside the window catches the attention of the witch looking radiant in the setting evening light. Outside, on the kitchen window ledge, a flock of pigeons has gathered. More and more pigeons filling the back garden with an incessant 'cooing'. 'What the crikey is all this?' she exclaims out loud. '

> *Directions mean nothing in the dark when you do not know where you are. To get to where you are going in life, know truthfully where you are right now.*

ANIMAL WELFARE

The pigeons flocking in the back garden has brought out the next-door neighbour from hibernation.

'Any chance ye might just feck off and mind your own business' cries out the Witch back over the neighbour's fence.

The neighbour responds in kind, 'get your pets in control' she roars 'or I'll have animal welfare out.'

The witch screams, 'shut your cake hole woman. Surely there is a takeaway open to keep you occupied?'.

After a few minutes, not a pizza delivery, but an orange van from animal welfare has arrived outside the house. The uniformed inspector looks intentional and approaches the house with meaning in his step. 'Listen, you can't be keeping flocks of pigeons in the back garden' he exclaims. The Witch's hair bristles at the dismissive tone of the inspector's voice. As you know, a Witch is not used to being spoken to by strangers and certainly not in this tone.

'Under EU Regulations, you need to have a licence for keeping birds in your garden' he prattles on.

The neighbour is now leaning over the fence watching with glee how this confrontation will develop.

The Witch is visibly agitated with the growing disturbance. She looks to the Inspector with his mouth open expectantly.

'These are not my birds, they arrived of their own free will and I have no control of where they choose to land' she says.

The inspector has removed his hat now and noticed the frog on the kitchen table in a dish of water.

'Sure, is it an animal farm that your running here?' he clacks.

The neighbour is delighted at the unfolding of the situation. 'You tell her' she cackles over the bowing fence straining to hold her balloon frame back.

The Witch has had enough. Walking calmly to the centre of the flock of birds, arms raised, she begins a chant.

'By all the power of land and sea, by all the might of moon and sun, as I do will, so shall it be'.

With that, the birds lift with a loud flocking of wings to the sky. Swirling around the Witch like a homing signal from a bird control tower. They fly skywards as though just released from a cage.

She turns back to the inspector with his mouth still open

'We are not an animal farm, we are frogsnotpigeons'.

> *Keep people in your life that motivate, encourage, inspire, enhance, and make you happy. If you have people in your life who are none of the above, just let them go*

THE WITCH, THE WIZARD, AND THE VIKING

The excitement had barely worn off from the visit of the animal welfare inspector and the Witch is just settling down to watch her usual binge of evening television, when her peace is rudely interrupted by the sudden arrival of her brother Naleek.

'Sister, sister!' she hears his urgent calling as the front door slams shut behind him.

'What now?' thinks the witch. Tired after the day's torrid events.

Naleek poked his head around the sitting room door, somewhat sheepishly.

'Sorry for dropping in like this but there is someone I want you to meet' barely containing his excitement.

'When do you ever apologise for dropping in unannounced anyway?' huffs the witch.

Naleek however, is oblivious to her sarcasm. He is already beckoning at someone in the hall to come in.

'Sister this is my new mott, Togram'.

The witch woefully gazes up as a Viking woman from the big boned Deise Tribe enters the room. Togram had a strange animalistic attraction about her. She had wild hair and gaps in her teeth but gawd she looked a powerful woman. She could easily be mistaken for a goalkeeper on a professional hockey team.

'Hello. Do you mind if I use your bathroom quickly?' I've been bursting since I left town'. Togram asks breaking the awkward silence.

'Eh yes through the door and to the left' says the witch momentarily snapping out of her pitiful trance.

'So, how are things going with the frog?' inquires Naleek making a desperate stab at conversation, 'What's its name?'

The witch looks down at her frog companion. 'His name is Robert'

'Robert!' exclaims Naleek. 'That is a coincidence, but how do you know?'

'He told me obviously' snaps the Witch defensively.

'Tell him your name frog' the Witch instructs the frog looking deep into its dull unseeing eyes.

'Ro-bert' croaks the frog, 'Ro-bert, ro-bert ro-bert'.

Naleek stares in disbelief at the frog as his sister smirks expectantly at him,

'See, his name is Robert, like I said.'

Suddenly a dawning realisation creeps up on Naleek's face. He suddenly understood his sister's recent moodiness and her attachment to this frog. There was meaning behind all of it. 'I'm happy you have him' said Naleek softly.

The Witch still watching the frog, was only half listening.

'You're happy I've what?'

'I'm happy you have Robert- for company after losing the pigeon'.

The witch stared at her brother with thinly veiled surprise. 'Um thanks I guess...'

She paused for a second.

'I'm happy you've found Togram too' she added softly. 'She might be handy if we ever start a local hockey league.'

The two siblings smiled at each other and basked in what they knew was a rare yet meaningful moment for them both.

When someone else's happiness is your happiness, that is love.

THE PIGEONS TEETH

'Togram – are you ready to go?' shouts wizard Naleek from the hallway. 'You are in the bathroom a long while'.

Getting no response, he glances to his sister, 'do you think we should intervene; she is already in there an hour?'

As you know, Viking women are fickle in their appearance and can take a bit longer than most on the makeup. However, the Irish Witch is getting impatient now with her visitors overstaying the welcome. It is a bit much to have your bathroom occupied by your brother's fancy woman for an hour, even if she is a Viking. She will have hair everywhere the Witch thinks to herself.

The Irish Witch does a gentle tap on the bathroom door.

'Are you done in there Togram?' calls out the Witch hesitantly and unsure on how that question might sound to anyone listening.

After a short time and no response, she places one hand softly on the door handle, and puts her ear against the door. In a moment, the Witch turns the handle and pushes the door open slowly. Like VERY slowly.

The small Viking Woman is cowering under the sink with her nail file in one hand and a bunch of feathers in the other.

'What are you doing woman?' asks the Witch from the safe vantage point of the doorway.

'Shhh…there is a flying rat in here' whispers Togram. 'It attacked me with its teeth flashing while I was doing my eyebrows'.

The Witch has now stepped into the room, slowly surveying the small space. The bathroom window is wide open and there are a hundred and twenty-seven lotion bottles from Boots everywhere. So, nothing unusual. However, Togram does indeed have a missing eyebrow. Not so attractive now she thinks, more like a cross eyed horse in a frock.

'I see no rat in here woman' calls the Witch, her sharp tone returning.

'Put away that nail file and fix yourself – I can't miss an episode of Love Island just because of you'.

Suddenly, from above the shower head, a frightened bird lifts to flight in the confined space. The lotion bottles are going in every direction and Togram screams a deafening pitch in a small space. The frightened bird sheds a path of loose feathers creating an even more chaotic scene.

Slowly, the Witch lifts her hand, palm open, and calls out. 'Be still, I command it, all be still'

And with that, time is frozen. With everything now motionless the Viking's mouth is open but silent for a change. Like a gaping cave

The Witch slowly opens the palm of her hand to reveal a startled pigeon not worse for losing a couple of feathers. Across the Witch's face, a growing smile, and a tear to her eye.

'After all this time, bird, I have forgotten how-to breath without you near'.

> *You cannot see unless you open your eyes. Sometimes, your soulmate is closer than you think.*

THE WITCH'S MONOLOGUE

Incredibly pleased to have the Pigeon back on the kitchen table. It is a break from the frog's single word nasal sentences, now relegated to an 'on-looker' from his bowl of water. I suppose if we were an amusement park, it could be called 'fun fair' dismissal.

The Witch's demeanour is thoughtful, reflective, and she is alone at the kitchen table with her two companions.

'I am happy you have returned pigeon; you were gone far too long my friend. The frog was no match for your company. I think it might have frog flu anyway for all the sniffling it does.'

The pigeon is motionless on the table except for the odd twitch that all pigeons have, or might have, in a similar situation.

The frog, keeping its mouth shut in case it ends up promoted from bowl to dinner plate, is watching nervously. It knows instinctively to be as quiet as possible. Except for the sniff now and then.

The Witch continues. 'If I could make amends Pigeon for what I've done. I feel a tightness in my chest like when the winter cold stops my breath. Without you I am an empty vessel with broken teeth'.

The Witch is now shaking like a leaf as though consumed with her loss and eager to try to put right, past wrongs. The Pigeon twitches silently on the table not sure where to look. Hard to know what the right move is when a magic woman is standing over you.

The Witch's voice is starting to shake with emotion. 'You came back because I called you. The maps are gone now and so are our footprints too. To get back now will take a lot more, and I'm not sure how'.

Daylight has ebbed away to evening. The Kitchen is now getting dim, creating an atmospheric glow in the room. As though questioning herself, she thinks, are we not more than just our surroundings? Surely as individuals, we are bright enough to outshine all the stars. What are we doing here, wishing our lives away, passing time, living day to day.

The Pigeon heaves its chest as though stretching or perhaps hiding a yawn, like when someone is disinterested in a conversation. The frog flutters in the water bowl with its eyeballs bulging intently trying hard to look as inedible as possible. Sniff.

True friendship is not just found. Its built.

THE TEARS OF A VIKING

The Simple Wizard Naleek grabs his coat and calls out to the Witch 'Think I will take the frog out for fresh air, down the pub for an hour while you are doing the dishes'.

Apparently, this was a common male practice in ancient Celtic Times, to exercise the animals.

'I'll come with you brother; it's been a while since I was out. The pigeon will be grand here by itself' she pipes back.

This is very unexpected, but she is out of the chair and already at the front door like a rabbit out of a trap.

As the sibling couple and the pocket frog arrive at the local bar, drinks are held mid-air for a few seconds as the couple enter under watching eyes.

'What can I get you?' the bar man enquires of the pair.

'A pint for me, a lemonade for the Witch and a saucer of water for the frog please'. Naleek answers with certainty in his voice.

The big Viking woman Togram and some of her clan are also in the bar. Togram approaches the couple as though preparing to scrum.

'Unusual to see you two out' she opens.

The Witches' hair bristles with disdain at the uninvited comment from this Viking who called her pigeon a rat previously. After looking the Viking woman up and down, 'I am entitled to be here as you are' the Witch interjects firmly.

'I wanted to ask you Witch if you could spare a few minutes for a reading' Togram asks cautiously.

'Perhaps I could offer you a Gin if that might persuade you?' she continues sheepishly.

Naleek responds on behalf of his sister. 'Sure, that would be fine Togram. Take a seat and we will join you'.

At a small round table that is typical in these rural pubs, the threesome and the pocket frog take a seat. It is an exceedingly rare event nowadays for a Witch to do a reading for the uninvited guest and certainly never a Viking in a public bar.

'I assume it's not a question on your hair or makeup. What is it that you'd like to know Viking?' starts the Witch with an air of indignance.

The Viking woman pauses. Her eyes glistening as she tears up slightly.

'Witch, you are not like everyone else. I know this because I am not either. Why will you not accept me for who I am?

The Witch pauses before responding softly.

'Stop looking for approval of others. Accept that you are good enough for you and you set yourself free to be who you are'

THE POSTMAN SHOULD ALWAYS RING TWICE

Ding dong...., the doorbell at the house chimes out. Who can that be? The Witch thinks to herself out loud. The doorbell has also upset the Pigeon on the table starting a chorus of cooing, like a feathered version of a guard dog.

'Shut up Pigeon' the Witch shouts back into the kitchen at the excited bird, who, although startled by the Witches voice, continues oblivious. Also, it is not a good idea to upset a Pigeon. They can be messy birds at the best of time.

The Witch opens the door to the postman. 'Eh, package delivery for the Witch?' he mutters in a questioning tone that reminds her briefly of George Clooney.

'About time – did it come from Mars?' she says flippantly.

Indifferent, the postman points to a signature location on his clipboard offering a sanitised pen to the Witch.

'By the way, I don't think they will fit you Witch, they are a small size and I doubt you could get one leg into them let alone two'.

The Witch stops mid signature.

'What do you mean by that?' lifting her stare from the clipboard to the postman's face, her eyebrows rising as though statically charged.

Uncomfortable by the Witch's stare, he takes a small step back trying to increase the social distance between himself and the Witch. 'I'm just saying, yoga leggings can be a tight fit'.

The Pigeon is flapping and cooing loudly now in the kitchen as though anticipating the rising tension of the conversation at the front door. 'And what size do you think I am?' the Witch asks. Her eyes starting to narrow, fixating her stare at the Postman's face. The Postman knows he is on dangerous ground at this point and that his next sentence could determine his future.

'Well, I'm sure I'm not qualified to answer that question, but....'

He does not get to finish the sentence. Like a scene from 'The Birds', the postman's arms are thrown in the air like a freestyle swimmer. Clipboard, pen and papers in the air, the Pigeon has launched a full-scale aerial attack on the Postman. As you can imagine, messy.

The Witch is also surprised by the intervention of the Pigeon. As she sees it, to defend her honour. She knows that you are responsible for how you react, no matter how you feel.

The Witch's upset at a 'slight' passed by a stranger, intentional or otherwise, dissipates. With one word from her, the Pigeon suspends the onslaught and resumes a position on her arm with no physical harm to the Postman except his ego.

Sometimes, it is hard to explain what you feel about a person, even a postman. It is about the way they take you to a place where no one else can. Never mention the fit of yoga leggings to a Witch.

SOMEONE LIKE YOU

The following night, the moon is high, and it is time to release the frog back to the pond in the garden. A dish of water on the kitchen table is no place for such a creature to exist and there is a real risk that he could become breakfast some morning. With a single candle on the table, and a chair wedged to the front door so as not to be disturbed. 'We are ready' she whispers to the green creature.

The frog is already in a state of heightened awareness and the Pigeon is just, well, looking on, not sure what to expect.

'I've searched a long time to find someone like you. You were everything I was looking for and I overreacted when I turned you into a frog. All a silly misunderstanding on my part, who's Doreen anyway?? Before I let you back into the pond to be with your own kind, I just want you to know, that if I could turn back time, I'd probably have given you a chance to explain yourself before cursing you forever and storming off. We had some great times together, but I realise that it can't be like this and it's time to let you go'.

The Pigeons chest is heaving as though it understands, and the frog has its mouth open as though waiting to catch some passing insect oblivious to the words spoken by the Witch. Now with tears streaming down her face.

'By all the power of land and sea, by all the might of moon and sun, as I do will, so shall it be, cast this spell and be it done'. Goodbye my friend.

A silence falls over the scene. The Witch's arms are raised towards the ceiling. The only sound is the intertwined beating of hearts from the Witch, the Pigeon, and the Frog. Imagine the sound of bongo drums played by a demonic monkey.

A sound in the garden breaks the bongo heart beats. The Witch turns slowly to the back window and appearing in the glass is a pair of dark eyes, cupped by hands, peering through the Kitchen window at the scene unfolding. No one moves. Then a crash sound from the hallway as the front door is forced, knocking the chair against the door to the floor.

The simple wizard Naleek appears at the doorway.

'Sister, we have been ringing the broken doorbell a while, Togram is at the back window. But look who I found on my way here – it is your old flame Robert; he has been trying to contact you for some time though Messenger and FrogSnap.'

The Pigeon Coos and the Witch turns back to the table to an empty water bowl that was previously occupied by a frog. A smile grows across her face and her watered eyes glisten knowingly in the candlelight.

A healthy relationship inspires you to be more of who you are, not require you to be someone else.

DOUBLE DATE SYNDROME

As a rule, Pigeons and Frogs are not left into restaurants unless they are on the menu or printed on a shirt. But then, a double date with a Viking Woman and a Witch who do not get on, could be an even bigger problem. In contrast, the other half of this double date, the newly returned Robert, and Simple Wizard Naleek, have no tensions and are deep in conversation about someone they do not know at another table. This is also an old Irish customary practice to talk about other people and find fault in people that you do not know.

'Are you glad that Robert is back in your life'? Togram asks the Witch trying to make some conversation.

'Maybe' the witch responds not engaging on the topic. 'Have you never heard of using hair conditioner?' she asks to Togram attempting to change the subject.

Togram flicks her peroxide straw like hair from her shoulder like an animalistic response to a threat.

'You have your man back, surely you must be happier to have a real person back in your life instead of that dumb Frog' snaps Togram. Her tone change is noticeable.

It is easy to tell when the Witch is irritated as her hair starts to grow outwards by itself as though charging electricity. Togram pokes again.

'He seems a nice man. Although not to my liking, a bit on the short side, like perhaps an extra from a Harry Potter movie'.

The Witch continues to lift food to her mouth although starting to look a little uncomfortable at the line of questioning.

The two lads are still talking and in deep conversation about the mystery of how water appears clear in a glass.

The Witch puts down her spoon and turns to the Viking woman seated beside her. Leaning slightly sideways, in a soft tone. 'Apart from your hair and clothing style, I have seen better fashion in a nursing home for the aged, we are not so different Togram'.

Togram leans closer. 'Witch, I am like a feather, strong with purpose yet light at heart and able to bend when needed. You are fixed and rigid, quick to judge others for their mistakes. Remember that it is much harder to pull yourself together than it is to fall apart. You should let the past go to move forward to the future'.

The two lads have returned to the present and stopped talking, suddenly aware of the tension rising. The Witch has turned back to her dinner but holding her spoon as though it could be used as a weapon. Robert reaches across the table to take the hand of the Witch in his.

Accepting his hand, she lifts her eyes to meet his as they connect in a moment that dissipates the emotional storm. Robert 'word mimes' to her across the table.

The act of forgiveness takes place in your own mind. It has nothing to do with anyone else.

LOVE IS IN THE AIR

The happy couples depart the restaurant at the stroke of midnight, and they walk out into the balmy summer night air. Unusual for this time of year in Ireland. Irritations between the Witch and the Viking Woman now forgotten, as each are consumed by their men. Hand in hand the foursome dance along the road like young children on a first school outing. The Witch cannot take her eyes off Robert, her eyes sparkling in the moonlight.

'I can't believe that you are back' she whispers softly to his ear.

Robert dances around the Witch like an overexcited puppy in the lane way without a care in the world.

No one pays attention to a distant engine noise that rumbles in the still night air as faint lights approach. The sound grows nearer as do the lights. Time stands still as the Number 6 bus suddenly rounds the narrow lane corner. The Witch is helpless, paralysed by fear. She tries to cry out in warning, but her voice is caught in her throat and refuses to leave. She can only watch as the bus bears down on her beloved. The bus driver desperately tries but fails to stop the bus in time. A thud sound and then silence broken only by the heart wrenching scream of a Witch that echo's her man's name across the night.

The Witch looks on at the scene unfolding under the moonlight, her hands clasped to her mouth as though to hold her breath. Numbed by the events, she sees only a frog splayed on the ground with a thread mark across its green skin back.

Thunder crashes through the night and lightning lights up the sky. The Witch's heart is racing and a thin film of sweat bathes her body, she hears screaming and realises the noise is coming from her. Her eyes open suddenly.

She is in bed. Recognizing her bedroom ceiling but still unsure what has happened, did it happen? where am I? where is Robert? Slowly turning her face to see Robert beside her motionless except for a gentle breathing sound that all men make. She tenderly brushes aside a downy pigeons feather from his cheek.

Her relief grows as a recognition of the reality dawns. Dreams are just that and not real. The Witch slips out of bed quietly to get a drink of water, her black silk, full length nightdress clings to her damp body. At the bottom of the stairs the pigeon is perched on the coat-stand head tucked tightly into its chest. At the kitchen sink where she last saw the frog, the witch realises that the frog is perhaps gone for good.

Sometimes, life is about risking everything for a dream that no one else can see. Live your life, do not look back, forgive...

A VIKING WEDDING

The Viking long ships are parked up along the river side and an impressive site with main sails blowing gently in the wind. The blue Pigeon emblem clearly displayed on the main sails, a sight to behold. Clearly a lot of expense gone into this wedding thinks the Witch to herself.

'I don't want to be here at this Viking Wedding' says the Witch as they enter the old Tower venue. 'They are a rude bunch who can't keep their hands to themselves at the best of times, let alone a family wedding of someone we don't know'.

Robert is trying to contain himself and not rise to the Witch's comments.

'We are here because Togram invited us to her cousin's wedding – so let us just enjoy it Witch'.

Togram and the Witch's brother Wizard Naleek approach.

'Welcome, so glad you could attend. Presume you left the broomstick around the back?' Togram mocks to the Witch.

Robert interjects quickly, 'there is a good turnout' he gestures back to the crowd assembled in the main hall.

'Ah sure what is a wedding without the gathering of the Viking Clans to celebrate the marriage of one of their own' postures Togram. Clearly proud of her heritage.

The Witch looks uncomfortable in these surroundings with many of a clan that are not her own folk. They look like sheep dippers who have not seen a shower for a long time she thinks to herself.

Some traditions do not change much. The Viking women are dancing in a circle around a stack of goatskin handbags with what appears to be dead sheep slung across their shoulders as wraps. The menfolk are circling the women, ready to pounce, waiting for one to separate from the safety of the herd.

Togram shouts over the music to make herself heard.

'It is a disappointment that the chief bridesmaid did not turn up and we have had the rescue helicopter looking for her. Presume that you have all heard that Doreen is missing for the last few weeks?'

Simple Wizard Naleek steps in closer to join the conversation. 'She is a lovely girl and would never have missed this occasion to wear a dead sheep on her shoulders' he interjects to the group. 'Perhaps you might ask your Pigeon to help?' he asks looking directly to his sister Witch, who, diverting her eyes, is now starting to look uncomfortable under cross examination.

'Maybe she has taken time off from her book career and gone to find herself?' offers the Witch sheepishly.

As the music changes to a slow set, a giant haystack of a Viking approaches and drops a dead horse offering at the feet of the Witch.

'You want to dance?'

Be happy. Be yourself. If other's around you do not like it, then let them be. Happiness is a choice that only you can make. Remember, life is not about pleasing everyone else.

THE WITCHES GATHERING

The annual gathering of local Witches is the highlight of the Witch calendar and this year is a paired back version due to social distancing. Our Witch has got her hair done for the occasion and a pair of high heels that could be used as a precision surgical tool. Robert is the unwilling driver but does not really have a choice and will collect a couple of the local frogsnotpigeons Witches on route to the venue.

With the car washed and cleaned, the Witch sends the group a FrogSnap message that they are on route and to mask up. The final departure is signalled.

'Are you sure this dress is alright on me?' the Witch asks as they leave the driveway.

'Its grand' he says, looking back over his shoulder as they reverse out.

'Not sure why you are bringing the Pigeon with you though?' he mutters but knows better not to repeat the question.

After a short while, Robert has got all the designated travellers into the car and is on the way to the venue. The car is filled with the different contrasting perfumery of the Witches, plus a Pigeon, and the elevated voice of each as they talk louder than the other. Witches have this uncanny ability to talk at the same time and yet still hold a conversation that no man can understand. The Pigeon is perched on the dash as though chairing a meeting of a gaggle of angry geese in the car.

As they approach the crossroads, the car slows to a stop as a local farmer crosses the section with a small herd of cattle – a common occurrence in this area.

'Why have you stopped Robert?' calls from the back seat and a silence for the first time in anticipated response.

'Because there is a herd of cows crossing the road' he responds slightly indignant at having to state the obvious with his head bobbing from side to side.

The Witches look to each other – 'I think I preferred Robert when he was a frog' calls out one of the Witches followed by a loud cackle.

'He still looks a little green behind the ears' calls another.

Then a deafening sound as all cackle at the joke cracked.

'Maybe you should have taken your broom sticks then' Robert mutters under his breath.

He opens his window and looks out across the fields for anything to draw his attention away from the provocation.

As the last of the cows cross the road, the last animal stops and looks to the car, perhaps also wondering what it is waiting for. Raising its head, it lets out a loud Moo. An indignant gesture to the car that is sharing its path. Eventually, it clears the road and Robert looks to select gear. A glance in his rear-view window and Robert is startled. He looks over his shoulder to the back seat to find it empty except for the Pigeon that has deposited white droppings all over the back seat.

> *Good people will give you happiness. Bad people will give you a lesson. The best people will give you memories. Men who give Witch's a lift must always hold their tongue or risk being left with the Pigeon.*

THE CRYSTAL BALL

On the last Sunday of the month, the Witch has a regular crystal ball slot down at the village café. It is well attended by the locals and a handy earner for the Witch. Today is no different, and there is a small group of locals down at the café waiting for their turn to ask the Witch questions of the Crystal Ball. With the ball in the centre of the table and the Pigeon perched on the chair, the first client is already in play.

'I see a woman who wants to talk to you' starts the Witch. 'Have you met someone new recently, that perhaps you we're not expecting?'

The client is one of the local farmers and does not have many of his own teeth left.

'Yes Witch, I've been trying out this new on-line dating app, and I think I may have got the hang of it now'.

The Witch lifts her stare momentarily from the glass ball to look at the man opposite her. Crikey, can't imagine he'll get too many 'matches' she thinks to herself.

'So, have you had many dates?' she asks as though speaking directly from her thoughts.

'Yer – not too bad' the man ventures back in a gruff voice. 'But nothing to get me past first base yet. I think it may be related to the fact that I don't look a bit like the profile picture I used'.

'Yah – that could do it alright' the Witch ventures back.

'Well, I have a new date tonight with a lady from the next village who says she has ploughing experience and all her own teeth'.

The Witch is back to staring into the glass ball.

'I see disappointment in your near future' she blurts out, 'perhaps you should adjust your expectations farmer'.

'Do you think so Witch? I've always fancied a woman who could throw a harpoon but thought I might be pushing it a bit'.

The Witch and the Pigeon continue staring into the crystal ball, as though willing the ball to speak or at least provide an image of something. A sudden light appears to grow within the ball itself. The Witch is startled. Appearing at the centre of the ball is a young woman's face. Thin, drawn, and with dark piercing eyes. Even the Pigeon is startled and has taken to a fit of flapping wings.

As the Witch withdraws her face back and then re-engages closer. Staring to the ball, the faint image of a female face is visible.

'It can't be – is that Doreen'? asks the Witch speaking aloud to the glass ball in anticipation.

Even the farmer is stunned into silence as the glass ball appears to be glowing in the centre of the table.

'Does she have a full set of teeth?' he asks.

Do not sell your dreams short for anyone. They are your dreams to live. Do not confuse your path with your destination. Just because its stormy now does not mean that it will not be sunshine when you get there.

SWITCHMAN'S SHADOW

Recovering from the months of social isolation brought about by the visitation of the Switchman, the Witch is taking her daily exercise with her Pigeon on her arm walking along the Greenway as she makes her way back towards the local village. Chanting words in her mind to create sensing magic, like in a form of mindfulness, she sees a dark shadow on a nearby hill that she must pass by.

As the Witch nears the pass, a hooded figure blocks her path as sometimes they do. And the Switchman speaks. Although angry with the Witch who has long defied him by wearing a mask in public and cost from him many lives.

The Switchman decides to hide his anger and instead speaks trickery to inquire her destination and offer her a gift to ease the travel. Reaching down, the Switchman picks a rounded smooth piece of glass from the nearby stream and offers it to the Witch.

'Take this glass Witch from my hand and keep it safe. For this glass has the power to summon those that have already passed. This I give you so that you may call on company to ease your loneliness along the way'.

The Witch knows that no magic has the power to return those already crossed over and wonders what game the Switchman wants her to play.

'Eh... no thanks. This dark power I did not ask for nor do I accept. It is as my people have always been and will continue' speaks the

Witch. Her brow narrows and her eyes focus on the image of the Switchman as though to stare it back into the shadows.

Visibly annoyed with the Witch and her perceived stubbornness, the Switchman drops the shiny glass to its feet and reaches to his cloak pocket to produce a wand fashioned of wood with thorns.

'Take this wand Witch and you will be the most powerful of all Witches of your tribe. You will stand shoulders above all your kind and be revered by all that hear the name Aradia or see your presence among the stars'.

'I need no reverence based on fear of my powers' responds the Witch. 'It is as my people have always been and will continue past this day and into the next'.

A spark of hidden anger escapes from the Switchman's eyes at the dissent of the Witch. A wave of rage passes across his face.

'You have taken from me Witch; the dues must be paid to restore balance to dark and light, to right and wrong, to good and bad. Some moons ago, you asked favour of dark powers to dispatch the Doreen out of misplaced jealousy and it was delivered. Now you must pay what is owed'.

The Witch knows in her heart of hearts that no Witch or Magic can defeat the Switchman. Instead she feigns cold and asks the Switchman if she may borrow his cloak to wrap her shoulders while they speak. The Switchman, in chivalry, removes his cloak and steps nearer to place across the shoulders of the fair Witch. In the moment of distraction, the Witch slips a hand to her pocket to grasp her alcohol spray and casts the spell of sleep on the Switchman. He falls to the side of the path and placing both hands under his cheek sleeps deeply as though a child in dream.

The Witch quickly moves past and continues her journey knowing that the Switchman is just sleeping and will soon return to claim his favour returned.

Recent events have shown that everything around us is

temporary. The ultimate measure of a person is not where they stand in moments of comfort but where they stand in times of challenge. Remembering that dawn always comes after the darkness.

FRAGILE LIFE

It is early dawn and the frogsnotpigeons have marched for many days on their return from the battle fields in defiance of the Switchman. Familiar tribal banners are visible along the path, barely moving in the early dawn breeze. The Witch looks to her side to look down on the Viking woman Togram. Her wild hair is a like a nest on her shoulders, heavily matted and colour contrasted partially compounded by the closing of hair salons.

'We should dismount near the gates and send whom we can, so to announce our return before approaching the gates' speaks the Witch in a solemn tone.

She raises an open hand sky wards to signal the intent to those behind. They need no further encouragement as the weary masked warriors stop willingly.

'Gather those that can – we need to see more than we can from here' shouts the Witch back to the followers.

Shortly thereafter, the hooded and masked group of frogsnotpigeons assemble. The group is noticeably smaller reflecting the loss of those that have fallen to the Switchman. The Witch casts the circle herself and those assembled begin to chant the summoning of the guardians of the four watch towers.

Togram, the Viking woman, does not partake in raising of magic. She is not of their kind. Her hands are rough, and she is as strong as ten men. Her face reflects the experience of many disputes with others and more often with herself. Despite this strength, her life force is not as strong, and she feels the early morning chills on her shoulders. Looking around her she sees the rolled up black cloak across the Witch's horse. Without a second thought, she unfurls the cloak not recognizing it as the Black Cloak stolen by the Witch from the Switchman himself. As Togram wraps the heavy cloak around her shoulders she pulls it tightly feeling momentarily relief from the chill. Nearby, Aradia has felt that something is not right. She glances over her shoulder to see Togram wrapped in the Cloak of the Switchman and cries out her warning that comes too late to help the Viking Woman.

Togram's relief from the chill is short lived. The Cloak envelops the burley Viking in darkness so black. Cries of the dead, of those past, and of loss rings loudly on the dawn air.

Suddenly Aradia feels her forearms tighten as someone, something so precious, has placed a weight into her arms.

And in her arms, the Witch feels the most delicate of treasures. It feels so fragile as though nothing else as fragile in this world, as though life itself was in her arms. Looking down, she sees the pale forehead of life itself, eyes closed, and hair blowing in the light breeze. Lips open slightly, as though to smile in the comfort of her embrace. A light radiates from the vision, like a lamp light that radiates even when we sleep. The Witch thought at that moment how delicate and precious is this light. One gust of wind is all it takes to blow it out....

The important things in life you cannot see with your eyes, only with your heart. In this time of shields and masks, what does your heart see?

REFLECTIONS

The Pigeon stretches its wings as though spoken words have just woken it from a dream. The challenges of the last few weeks have taken a toll. Social isolation, daily death reports, collective grief, and a future of uncertainty. The Witch is home alone with her bird and sadness. Not for the first time. A sudden sound from outside startles them both, and in the mirror, she sees the image of the hooded Pan standing behind her in the doorway. A welcome distraction she thinks, but it has been more than two moons and so much has happened. The image of Pan moves closer so that the Witch can almost feel his presence.

'So, you have returned safely'? speaks Pan in a casual, almost dismissive tone.

'Yes' she responds. 'But not without many losses along the way, including the Viking woman who sneezed one night and mistakenly borrowed the Cloak of another for her comfort'

Pan looks down on the sorrow of the Witch as she turns her eyes to the wooden tabletop and the scratching bird who seems more agitated than normal.

'Perhaps the mistake was not the woman's but yours. Afterall, she borrowed the Cloak from you that was not yours to lend' speaks Pan.

The Witch purses her lips tight on the sound of this half-truth. She feels a hurt tense over her as the uninvited judgement is delivered upon her. The Pigeon flaps and begins to coo loudly as though to remonstrate against the harsh words spoken by the visitor.

The Witch glances to the bird, as its sound draws on her attentional focus. The mirrored image moves closer in the moment of distraction to stand directly behind the Witch. Closer than comfort and even social distancing permits.

'Some people are never satisfied where they are' she hears spoken in a deep voice. 'They chase after no one and nothing' speaks the hooded man.

'Some care what they have and where they are' responds the Witch. 'They spend their time on what is precious to them and value what they have. Instead of chasing gold they focus on the silver lining'

'Then they are more fortunate than they know' speaks the hooded reflection of Pan.

The Witch watches the mirror reflection and sees the boned hand of Death reach into the cloak pocket to withdraw the knife of ethalmus. Its blade glints in the mirror as it rises quickly over her shoulders behind her. Instantly, she realises she has been tricked easily and moves to avoid the impending strike.

A silence envelops the Ménage à trois. The small room is like a shaken snow globe of white feathers that fills the air. The Witch sees bright red pooling, escaping the table surface and drip to the tiled floor. Beside the blood, the Pigeon lies motionless in its own ebbing life pond. Behind her, where once stood the hooded image of missed hope, the shadow of loss is all that remains.

Sometimes, you must let go of the picture of what you thought it would be like and learn to find joy in the story you are living.

WISHING ON STARS.

'I can hear your thoughts' speaks Robert softly.

The Witch does not look up, instead focuses on the small pale frog.

'Perhaps we are destined to be where we are' he continues. Speaking slightly louder to assert that the Witch has heard him.

But still she resists his efforts to converse. The Witch's eyes narrow as she stares intently at the ailing frog before her.

Robert does not give up so easy. Instead slides up beside the Witch and sits himself beside her pushing aside the dish of water. Eventually, she turns her eyes towards him looking up through her wild straw like hair.

'There is a lot of other empty seats' she blurts sarcastically.

Robert does not take the provocation. Instead reaching into his little pocket, he lifts a small vial and places it on the counter-top before the Witch. The Witch's gaze turns to the curiosity.

'Make a wish' he says pointing towards the small vessel.

The Witch thinks momentarily, her mind processing the meaning of what she hears and sees. Hesitant, the Witch's mind races of thoughts about unimaginable wealth, beauty, power, the kind of things that real-world people wish for. Can this be for real, she wonders as she stares at the small vial placed before her.

'Take it Witch' reaffirms Robert. 'This is the gift that I promised two moons ago before the lockdown. Wish for anything that you want, that all will be right with you. But be careful what you wish for. Only the person that releases the Genie may call on its magic'.

Slowly, the Witch leans forward and takes the stoppered vial into her hand. Rolling the smooth dark glass between her fingers and thumb, the Witch feels the contained power in the small object and hesitates in the possibilities.

Behind her, what sounds like hoofed feet on floorboards, clip clop across the room as though a large horse approaching. Both turn quickly. And from over her shoulder, the Witch sees a Viking woman approach. Her broken tooth smile is wider than any farm gate. The Viking leans forward over the Witch's shoulder. The vial comes loose from the Witch's hand and rolls across the countertop as though trying to escape. In doing so, the vial stopper departs from its home and rolls helplessly away releasing the contents of the small vessel.

Both scramble to catch the rolling vial in vain as it falls to floor and shatters in many pieces like stars on a black slate floor. A green mist rises from the vial taunting those that have disturbed its inhabitant.

'What is your Wish – Speak it now' booms the Genie.

'I wish I could find my perfect match' stutters the Viking woman. Not finishing her sentence aloud. Before a large puff of smoke and Robert is gone. Leaving only the Witch sitting at the bar.

Stars in the sky carry the wishes of many. For some, they come as falling stars to earth. For others, they stay in the sky forever, never gone, always in sight, never landing until the Watcher turns his eyes away in resignation. Such is the life of people who wish their future as the present passes them by unnoticed. Sometimes, we confuse what we wish for with what is already.

THE WISHING WELL

High up in the mountain near the Witch's home village, there is a magic wishing well that is protected by strong faire magic. Each year at the longest day, many of the local people attempt to climb the steep mountain to reach the well and ask of the guardians of the mountain to grant them a wish. Locals say that the wishing well must be reached the same day to be of effect and many attempt the climb although few will reach the well by sundown.

Waiting for daybreak at the bottom of the mountain, three witch crones of the frogsnotpigeons coven, each share their own tale of sadness, disappointment, and sorrows with the other. As though competing to have the most sorrowful story and taking solace from the sadness of each other's story.

The first crone speaks her story of aging too quickly and how her once beautiful golden hair now has grey roots coming through. She spoke of comparing herself to others of youth with their golden hair, soft skin, and spindle legs in yoga pants. Her wish if granted is that she could have her youthful appearance back so that she can be happy again.

The second crone speaks her story of how an evil sorcerer, her mother in-law, cast a spell so that no matter what she did, it was never good enough. She spoke of unfounded criticism for her cooking and her housekeeping and even how she brought up her own children. Her wish if granted was that she could be unburdened of the guilt of failure and be satisfied again.

The third crone speaks her story of how she was recently dumped by her boyfriend, whom she loved dearly, for a younger model.

She spoke of her grief and longing every time she saw them together in the local village. Why should they be happy together? Her wish if granted, was that she could win her man back and live happy ever after.

Each feeling sorry for the other, the crones resolved to help each other get to the top of the mountain thinking that surely the three working together had more of a chance than each alone.

As the first ray of sun opened the day, the group move forward to the base of the mountain. The path is steep and loose stones underfoot makes the hike up the mountain path difficult. Each of the crones tie their long robes together to form a makeshift rope of linen between them that helps to pull one another up along the mountain path. After hours of climbing higher up the mountain path, the screams of excitement turn to disappointment and start to ebb as other climbers behind surrender to the physical effort and return back down dejected, resigned to postpone their attempt to reach the Wishing Well another year.

The three crones, each tied to the other, eventually reach a large rock formation that prevents further access along the path. Among these giant boulders lives a swollen goblin that has lived so long alone that the loneliness has made it blind with anger. Sensing the presence of the three crones, it calls out the following words.

'To pass here, you must show me your pain for those who cannot see.'

Each of the crones cast their worst spells and curse the blind goblin to no avail. It was quickly apparent that spells had no effect on the eyeless goblin seated stubbornly to block their path forward. As each crone exhausted their spell casting, they fell to their knees in despair. They were so upset that tears streaming from their eyes formed a pool on the ground before and around the blind goblin.

Then the blind goblin bent over and placed its lips into the pond of salty tears drinking from the pool of drama before it. After not so long, the goblin wiped its mouth. Satisfied, it dragged itself aside on its fat ass and disappears back into the mound of boulders.

The crones of course are delighted and resolved to press on to the mountain top that was now in sight. Near to the summit, they come across a flat stone in the ground scratched deeply with the following words.

To pass here, you must pay me the wages of your labour.

The three crones look to each other as none of them has brought a purse or coinage with them. 'Flipping Nora' – cries out the first crone, 'there is no one here to make us pay, let us go through'.

Each of the Crones looks to the other and through the absence of any other plan, all agree to drive on with the climb.

Hours pass on the shale stone climb, one foot after the other, deeper into the dusty shale stone. The slipping and sliding under foot made the effort useless as though treading quicksand. And the scratched words remain staring back up at them through the shale. One of the three crones decided to undo herself from the tethered robes and scramble hard alone.

She pumps her strong legs hard in the shale that cut her ankles. She uses her hands to grab anything she can that she might climb through.

'I refuse to be beaten' she cries aloud, wiping the sweat from her brow.

The beads of sweat run from her forehead, down her strong back and drip to the grey shale. And the more she sweat, the more it glistened on the dusty shale ground until the wretched scratched words faded from sight.

Removing her robe to use as a rope, the hard-working crone reaches behind and with great effort, drags her two companions up past the sliding shale path. Delighted by overcoming the second obstacle, they commit to achieving their goal and reach the Wishing Well before darkness fall. As they approach the Wishing

Well in dusk light, they arrive to a small stream that crosses their path. The clear water burbles fast across the smooth stones that looks like glass below the surface. One of the flat smooth stones has an inscription carved deep.

To pass here, you must pay me the savings of your past.

This time, the three crones drop to the ground in despair and ponder the meaning of the message. Many hours pass and the sun slips lower to the edge of the horizon. Each fall silent in their own thoughts. Memories of happy times fill their minds. The first crone remembers how she had danced and laughed in the corn fields and how happy she was. She thought about her true friends who never judged her and accepted her for who she was regardless of appearance. The happy thoughts made a broad smile come across her face and she looked around to see her companions share that smile.

In that moment each of them realised that their own hardships in life made them who they are today. The three crones hugged each other tight in happiness and in doing so released the sadness that had brought them together on this mountain path. And with the display of love for each other, the message on the stone washed away with the water and disappeared. The three crones crossed the stream and finally reached the wishing well. As each of the three crones peer down into the dark water at the bottom of the deep well, a silence of contentment falls across each of them.

The first crone realised that beauty was in her own mind and that youthfulness comes from within. She resolves to live her life in the moment and stop wishing away time.

The second crone realised that the fear of failure she carries was of her own making. She resolved to make her own effort to build inner confidence and not listen to others criticism.

The third crone realised that losing her lover to another was not of her making and that she had escaped a life with someone not worthy of her love and trust.

The three crones turned and holding hands skip and laugh going back down the mountain path grateful for the new gifts they have received for the rest of their lives.

None of them realizing that there was no magic in the dark water at the bottom of the well.

Stop setting yourself on fire for those who want to watch you burn. Who you are is self-determined only by you and not by others.

THE FINAL CALL.

Why are we meeting in the village hall?' snorts one of the frogs-notpigeons crones. The Witch, Aradia, glances back at the source of the question from one of her crew as though to dismiss with her eyes. Inside, there is a strong smell of dampness that hangs thick in the air. Aradia stops in the centre isle and looking down one of the empty pews, points her crooked finger to signal to the group behind that this is their place to sit. Each obediently slides along the polished bench so that the row is filled. The dim light of the hall broken only by islands of candlelight that causes shadows to dance across the walls towards high ceilings. The Witch takes her place at the front row. She removes her tall black hat and places it beside her on the wooden bench. Two rows behind, the frogsnotpigeons gathered, follow their masters lead, and in unison, remove their pointy hats and face masks.

As others start to file into the hall, every other row of seats starts to fill up behind the Witch while maintaining social distancing. These are mostly the village folk, non-magical souls, who live their day to day existences measured only by the number of chores performed daily.

The Witch glances over her shoulder as the sacred hall fills. She holds to the outer edge of the pew determined that she will keep the aisle seat. 'Excuse me dear' sounds a crakety old crone that has arrived at the Witch's front seat row. The Witch looks up to the time worn eyes of an old wizen crone. Her weathered face is partly concealed by her long and unkept grey hair that has not seen a hairdresser in a long time. 'Would you mind?' she asks again with a gentle signal from her walking stick. In her mind the Witch wonders why the oldie cannot just sit somewhere else.

However, her spoken words are different.

'Yes of course, I will slide right along, and you can take my warmed seat' she smiles as she slides along the polished bench. Her long dark cloak pulled tight.

And so, the old Crone took the place at the top pew beside the youthful Witch Aradia.

At the top of the hour, the main doors are closed and the mutterings of the assembled still to silence. Well almost. The ancient Crone leans in towards Aradia as though an old tree about to fall.

'Loan me your warm cloak dear to keep the chill of this place away' she wheezes in a broken voice. The Witch rolls her neck twice as though a power lifter about to perform the snatch lift. 'Do you need it old crone?' she thinks.

But her spoken words are different.

'Sure, no problem' and she pushes the black cloak from her shoulders and places across the boned shoulders of the old woman beside her.

'Now, that will keep you warm' she says as she pushes back in the bench to sit upright. As moments pass, there is a strange quiet and the Witch hears her own breath. Breathing deep through her nose, she fills her lungs with the damp air before exhaling forcefully that she hears clearly over the quietness. Strange, I can no longer hear the oldie wheezing she thinks as she turns to glance to her left at the old crone beside her.

On turning, Aradia notices that the old crone is smiling staring into space. Her wheezing no more.

'Are you alright?' asks the young Witch.

The old crone turns slowly and returns the cloak to the Witch.

'Thank you, I shall not need it anymore' she whispers before closing her eyes for the last time.

And a sadness suddenly descended over the Witch as thoughts of time lost and missed opportunities fill her mind. The Witch turns and cups her hands around those of the old crone. She hears a whisper in her mind calling.

Some are pre-occupied with the thought that happiness is in the next place, the next job or with the next partner. Until you give up the idea that happiness is somewhere else, it will never be where you are. Live for today, tomorrow will find you soon enough. Sometimes, we have no choice but to let go of what is lost or gone

THE SECOND COMING

During this time of pandemic and the second coming of the Switchman, the people of the land had become frustrated with social distancing and the ever-changing demands of the village council. The village mayor had become afraid of losing his influence over the people and started looking for more and more strange ways to keep his influence intact. He resented the respect that the Witch got from the villagers and felt demeaned by her magic and her powers that she used to some effect holding back the Switchman.

The mayor changed his advisors frequently and started to surround himself with those that agreed with his delusional conspiracy theories that sought to undermine the Witch's influence while at the same time, giving the Village mayor more power over his ever changing cabinet. One of his new advisors who had arrived in from out of town, whispered to the mayor's ear that he should take the power of the Witch for himself and diminish the influence of the Witch over the common folk of the Village. Eventually, the mayor started to agree with this new advisor and listened more and more. He decided that he will learn how to do magic for himself and issued an instruction to hire a Wizard who will teach him the dark ways. Of course, none of the real Wizards or Witches in the local area were too bothered with the job advert and thought it just a joke. So, no real Witch or Wizard came forward for the vacancy.

However, after months of lockdown and social restrictions, many had lost their jobs and people were desperate for new career paths and applied for anything that came up. One young lad in the next village, saw the opportunity and decided that he would apply for the role. Despite that he had zero magic powers and met none of the hiring criteria. His rationale was that many people get into power roles with no experience so why shouldn't he.

However, even this chancer lad was surprised when he got the call to be interviewed for the mayor's magic instructor role. He dusted off an old cloak and figured he should at least look the part for the interview, but never expecting to get the job.

Arriving at the Village Hall for interview, the lad decided that he would big it up. He claimed to be a massive Wizard from the neighbouring village. He performed a few slights of hand tricks for the naïve mayor and was immediately hired to the position of Chief of Village Magic and Private Magic Instructor to the Village Mayor.

The lad deftly negotiated his starting salary way above what he previously earned in his last role as glass collector at the local inn. He also secured a sign on bonus that he needed to purchase his box of magic tricks for the mayor. All of these demands the dumb ass mayor provided to the young confidence trickster delighted with his new appointment.

With cash in his pocket, the young lad next needed to figure out what trick he could teach the mayor. Of course, he had already heard tell of the local Witch Aradia and decided this was his next call. Although a little nervous, the lad was confident and after making his visit appointment, called to visit the local Witch.

On entering the small cottage, the Witch Aradia greeted him with her elbow in compliance with social distancing rules. She treated him as she would any other paying visitor and vouched the young lad to take a seat at her kitchen table where she has done many readings before. The Witch looked the young lad up and down and wondered what this lad could want from her. In-turn, the young lad also looked the Witch up and down and wondered what kind of a Witch keeps a Pigeon on her kitchen table.

'Speak boy, tell me what you want from me' speaks the Witch as she settled into the session.

'I am the Mayor's new Chief of Magic and I want to purchase spells' he said in a confident tone.

'Oh, really. If you are the Chief of Magic, why do you need to purchase spells from me?'

'I don't. But I was told that you have what I need' he spoke with slight irritation in his voice at the question from this village Witch.

With that, he placed before the Witch and the Pigeon a bag of coin he had obtained from the mayor.

The Witch thought carefully for a minute and then placed a pointy hat on the table in front of the young man.

'You should start with this magic hat of tremendous power. But heed what I say, young Chief of Magic, power in the wrong hands can bite those who don't treat it with respect due.'

The young man eagerly picked up the hat before him and promptly placed it on his head.

'Like many things in life. It will need some practice' said the Witch. 'When you are worthy to hold such a gift. That is when it will come to you'

With that, the young lad pushed the small bag of coins across the table to the Witch. Stepping to his feet he decided that this was a good deal and concluded the meeting. Quickly exiting the Witch's home, he set off to make a fresh start the following day with his new employer.

FIRST DAY ON THE JOB

On the morning, the young Chief of Magic arrived at the mayor's office and promptly presented his new magic hat to the mayor.

'This is a Witches hat of tremendous power that will make you a great magician. It will only work when you are worthy and ready to hold such power' he announced to the sullen looking mayor.

The mayor had a glint in the corner of his eye as he eagerly took possession of his new powerful magic hat. Examining the tall pointed hat, he determined that this was indeed a powerful tool and that he was to be the most powerful mayor in the village and will use his magic to get the respect of all the villagers.

Every morning, the Chief of Magic and the mayor walked the garden courtyard where they waved their hands and shouted nonsense to the sky. The young Chief of Magic was super careful to throw in a few tricks for his employer that he could maintain the confidence of the old man in his magic ability. And so, he kept his job and got paid handsomely for the task at hand.

One such morning of practice, the Chief of Magic and the mayor were dancing around a tree in the courtyard and cursing the leaves to fall on command when a loud cackling sound disturbed their exercise. To the other side of the courtyard the pair spotted what appeared to be a cleaning lady who was falling around holding her sides with laughter at the sight of the Mayor in the ridiculous pointy hat. The arrogant mayor could not contain his anger at being laughed at by one of his serving staff and turned his dissatisfaction towards his Chief of Magic.

'Do you think me a fool?' he roared into the face of the young lad.

'I have had enough of this practice and tell you I'm ready to accept the power of the hat now!'

The young Chief of Magic wiped the mayor's spittle from his face into his sleeve and determined that time was against him. He tried in vain to soothe his masters impatient rage but to little effect. The laughing of the cleaning lady had stung the pride of the mayor that nothing could soothe him except proof of his own magic capability.

'Tomorrow,' said the mayor, 'I will invite all of the villagers to the town hall so that they can see my magic for themselves and respect me for who I am.'

The young Chief of Magic could see that there was no dissuading the mayor from his course and decided that agreement with his master's wish was the only safe option. With no more to be said, the mayor stormed off back into the village hall leaving the young Chief of Magic wondering what fate lay ahead for him. He turned to see the cleaning lady resume her sweeping on the other side of the courtyard and determined that this wretch was the source of his calamity. Striding meaningfully towards the woman, he kicked the broom from her hands. 'You have cost me dearly crone!' roared the young Chief of Magic. 'How dare you laugh at me and disturb my important work!' The young cleaning lady looked up into the face of the young boy and smiled into the red face of anger. 'How dare you even look at me – old Crone, do you know who I am?' continued the Chief of Magic.

'If you do not know who you are – perhaps I can ask around for you?' replied the cleaning lady slightly bemused by the antics of this young whipper snapper.

With that, the young Chief of Magic raised his arm, set to strike the cleaning lady. Without flinching, the young girl raised a finger on her right hand and a strong swirl of wind entered the enclosed courtyard. The gust was so strong as to take the leaves from tree that swirled around the young Chief of Magic like a tornado. The young lad waved his arms in the cyclone to cover his face from the damp leaves that circled him. As the gust of wind subsided the courtyard floor was covered with the damp leaves. The young Chief of Magic stared at the cleaning woman. 'You will help me tomorrow with the mayor's practice of magic or I will denounce you as a turned Witch that has disrupted the important learning of the mayor!'

The young cleaning lady smiled at the Chief of Magic and assured him that she would do everything she could to help. The Chief of Magic told the cleaning lady that she was to hide the following morning in the courtyard and that when the mayor performed his call to the sky that she would use her magic to call to the wind as she had just done.

The cleaning lady however was slightly perturbed with the plan and decided to make the plan known to the village Witch, Aradia, for fear that the plan might go wrong, and she could be target of the mayor's dissatisfaction. Aradia listened to the cleaning lady's story and determined that she will provide necessary assistance to ensure that all went to plan.

Well, sort of. It would not be the plan of the 'Chief of Magic' but instead a new plan formulated in the mind of the Witch Aradia.

THE DEMONSTRATION

On the morrow, Aradia and her sisters had disguised themselves well. Joining as part of the cleaning staff and took up a hiding place in the courtyard ready for the mayor's display of magic. Aradia watched from her vantage point as the local villagers started to assemble in the courtyard. Near the appointed time, the village mayor appeared and took a place on the assembled stage with his Chief of Magic by his side.

As the Mayor stepped forward to the podium, he placed the old pointy hat on his head and waved his hands in the air to greet the assembled.

'I know we are all tired of this pandemic business. But today I plan to demonstrate my magic powers.'

The crowd watched on not sure what to expect. But it is difficult to read facial expressions of those wearing face masks.

'I shall firstly wave my hand and call out to the powers of the watchtowers to make themselves known to us 'cried out the mayor. Waving his hands as though conducting an orchestra he recited a couple of indiscernible words. At the same time, the Witch at the back of the courtyard lifted her arms to the sky and drew breath across the assembled people. A light breeze fluttered through the courtyard so that those with caps were forced to hold them in place. Great was the astonishment of those gathered and each whispered admiration to the other. Remember, these are but simple folk not used to much. A loud round of applause from the crowd followed for the happy mayor in his ridiculous pointy hat.

'Next, I shall make a spell that will magic a food banquet that we may all take our fill'. Again, waving his hands, the mayor ranted off a few words that made no sense to anyone. The Witch looked on with some amusement but had already decided that she no longer wished to play. When nothing happened, the mayor repeated his nonsense and waved his hands even harder. The crowd began to whisper and then laugh at the antics of their foolish mayor in a pointy hat on the stage before them.

As the mayor waved harder and harder, his face became redder and redder. Deciding enough was enough he doubled over himself to try and catch his breath all the while the assembled crowd nearly laughed their heads off. Eventually, the mayor summoned enough reserves and turned to his Chief of Magic. 'How dare you make a fool of me' he screamed. 'How very, very, dare YOU!'

'But, but, it was not my fault' stuttered the Chief of Magic as he pointed his finger over the heads of the assembled crowd to the hooded figure standing at the back dressed like a cleaning maid.

'She is a Witch!' exclaimed the young and not so wise Chief of Magic still pointing his finger.

'You must catch her and make an example of this Witch. She would dare to interfere with the leadership of the mayor'.

The foolish mayor was now looking in the direction of the hooded woman. Perhaps the only person not laughing at him. He squinted his eye and pointing an eyebrow in the Witch's direction as though determining his next course of action. He snapped the ridiculous hat from his bald head and he quickly cast it from the stage to the ground realising now that it was, well, just a silly hat. He must have revenge and it must be public revenge to quite the laughing and sniggering. The mayor called his guard and instructed them to lock the courtyard gates that no one will leave or enter. The crowd assembled, sensed the anger of the mayor and the laughing was replaced gradually with concern.

The mayor caught hold of the young chancer Chief of Magic and dragged him from the stage to stand in the centre of the courtyard. The crowd made a perfect circle around them although now crowded into the smaller space. Shoulder to shoulder they stood. Laughter changed to mutterings of concern. Should we be this close in a closed space?

The mayor forced the young Chief of Magic harshly to his knees before him. And the mayor was still angry waving a fist in the face of the young smart-ass boy who had taken his money so easily. The mayor started to realise his own foolishness. With the arrival of this COVID 19 and the subsequent lockdown and then the social distancing measures imposed by the government, he felt his influence diminish. He had listened to the frustrations and complaints from the village folks and felt powerless to help them. They seemed more interested in 'nature' and 'going for walks' while all the time he did nothing except eat more and watch television. After all, he surmised, I am the Mayor of this village. I should be able to say what goes on in my own village. Surely.

THE REPRIMAND

The crowd slowly parts as the guard brings the hooded woman to the cleared space at the centre where she stood before the Mayor and the chancer boy still cowering at the mayor's feet. 'This is the Witch that has made us all look foolish' cries the boy so that all who can hear. 'She has disguised herself well among us. We need to make her learn a lesson and show her that we are not sheep'.

The Witch slowly lifts her head to look upon the overweight Mayor and his young liege. Her face is still partly covered by her face mask but her piercing eyes speak for themselves from within the darkness of her hood.

She speaks. 'You are a foolish man to think that you can buy the gifts of magic.'

'Do you know who I am?' responds the Mayor. His arrogance still intact.

'I know you. And I know your kind.' speaks the Witch. 'You have placed many people at risk to soothe your own ego.'

'What are you talking about? Take off the mask that I can see your lips speak these words!'

'You are a dumb ass and still cannot see what you have done' she screams back.

The surrounding ordinary folk huddle ever closer together and watch the events unfurl as though a favourite episode of a soap opera.

The Witch turns her attention to the young confidence trickster still on the ground and commands him to stand. 'You are a greedy young man who thought to make gain at the cost of the public purse with your parlour tricks for fools'.

'You are just a cleaning maid' he responds. His stubborn confidence still intact. 'Perhaps when I had the chance to smack you down, I should have taught you a lesson that you might know your place.'

'I already know my place' responds the Witch. 'And I am no cleaning maid for the likes of you.' Bristling. Quickly she draws her hand from a pocket and strikes the young man across his face. The strike is well made. The boy recoils quickly but then quickly jump to his feet to face off the Witch before him. His eyes bulge with anger. He is not a man that is used to being chastised by a woman.

The Witch holds her ground as the angry young man appears to exercise his face muscles as he thinks his next move. The surrounding crowd become the audience to the match off. Huddled close, there is a repressive mood among the people who do not have the choice to leave. In that moment of anticipation silence, there is a loud sneeze from one of the crowd. Eyes dart fleetingly in the direction of the sound. But it is not a concern that registers as important for any of these simple folks. But there are other pressing matters unfolding here as a young Witch is about to teach the confidence trickster a lesson. Like perhaps a group of football supporters, the crowd now begins to jeer the combatants to act. Go, Go, Go, Go, Go.... Rings out from the crowd.

The young man wipes his sleeve across his running nose like a child from kindergarten. In the moment, the Witch looks beyond her unequal opponent, to see a tall hooded man standing on the once vacant stage. Around him a strange light emanates out and across into the crowd. For the moment at least, all attention is now back to the stage and this strange appearance of the tall hooded man. How did he get in here with all the doors locked? What is this light coming from him? These are the thought questions circulating among the bystanders.

The tall hooded man is now at the mayor's podium. 'So glad of you to invite me back into your small world' speaks the Switchman.

The Witch, still behind her face mask, recognises the voice as he continues speaking.

'I knew eventually that you would call me back. Masks and social distancing are but ploys of the powerful to subdue the weak. But not you. Beautiful people who are assembled here at the call of your Mayor to a closed space without masks or social distancing. Perhaps a Golf Society outing for politicians? Anyway, I congratulate you on your independent thought to express your free will to choose'.

The crowd withdraws as far as they can in the confined courtyard. A sense of uncertainty and even fear goes through the group as though a wave arriving to the shore. The Witch is standing alone now. The Switchman turns his focus to the lone standing female before him in the centre of the courtyard.

'Ah... a face-masked Witch' he drolls out sarcastically from the podium.

'You were sent packing the last time and so will it be this time' shouts the Witch.

A laugh rings out around the courtyard that echoes in the closed concrete space.

A WITCH'S DANCE

Aradia, the Irish Witch knows deep down that she is no match for the Switchman alone. He comes back stronger each time. There is no fear. He is strong and his strength grows with each visitation as he adapts and learns the ways to contain and defeat him each time. Raising both her arms to the dark sky she begins her summon call to assemble with her, the coven of frogsnotpigeons. Together we are stronger. 'Earth and Water, Wind and Fire, as I do will, so shall it be.' Rings around the courtyard accompanied only by the mocking laugh of the Switchman from his temporary podium.

In a cloud of smoke, the Witch stands. Momentarily out of sight as the white smoke billows into the sky. Five of the frogsnotpigeons maidens step forward from the smoke to assemble behind their master Aradia.

'Ah good... the rest of your crew are here as-well' calls the Switchman, unphased by the assembled group of hooded Witches. Stepping down from the podium the Switchman makes his way down the wooden steps to stand before the ensemble of women. Each hooded woman stands small compared to the broadness and height of the Switchman. Carefully, he circles the group of women like a prowling lion looking for a weakness or dissent in the group. Who will break first he wonders?

As the Switchman comes full circle, he now stands directly in front of Aradia.

'I like this game' he retorts. 'Let us begin our dance Witch.'

The Witch Aradia feels a lightness about her as the Switchman comes nearer. Her eyes close as she experiences a sensation that she has felt before. She senses that time has stopped, and a silence falls around her. Darkness and silence befall the young Witch. Waiting for something to happen that does not arrive, the Witch slowly opens her eyes to find herself transported and standing alone in a distant location surrounded by fields of barley. Scanning the horizon, she sees a farmer ploughing the adjacent field using large plough horses not seen in this area for many years.

'What is this place?' she whispers under her breath.

'This is the time of the first coming' answers the Switchman standing beside her in the field.

'Why have you brought me here?' asks Aradia.

'This is where we first met – where it all began. Do you not remember?'.

The Witch looks closer as the farmer ploughing nears. His face is familiar and instantly she has recognized her long past grandfather. A tear escapes from the corner of her eye as the lone ploughman and his horse pass near-by unaware of their presence in the field.

'My grandfather passed a long time ago' she says quietly.

'Yes, I know. It was in the spring of 1917' is the cold response.

'I do not understand why you have brought me here'.

She feels the touch to her arm by the Switchman and they are instantly transported to another place. A densely populated city with a skyline of tall high rises of concrete. The crowds mull through the city scape seemly oblivious of each other as they go about their mundane existence.

'We knew that we would have history between us from the first time that we touched' speaks the Switchman in an unnerving but gentle tone.

The Witch turns to look on the face of the Switchman to see a young man. Not what she expected of death and disease and suffering. Again, he reaches and touches her arm and she once more senses transportation. This final time, the miss matched couple arrive to stand at a campfire on a beach.

'You make the stars shine brighter. Like they are ours. Like there is no one else in the World' whispers the Switchman closer than comfort to the Witch's cheek. 'Take down that face cover that I can see your radiance one more time'.

Intoxicated in the moment, the Witch lifts her hand to her ear to lift down the face covering to release her breath and breathe fresh once more. She breathes the warm salt air deep. Filling her lungs to capacity and holds for a second. She exhales slowly and closes her tired eyes.

SENESCENT CELLS

As the Witch opens her eyes slowly, she realises that she is not where she expected to be. Where the dull white bedroom ceiling should be, there is instead a black ceiling of stars. In fact, it is not just the ceiling but the entire room that is stars.

Slowly standing to her feet on an invisible plane, the Witch finds herself surrounded by constellations as though she is floating in space. There is no fear. The Witch is in awe at the wonder of the universe that surrounds her on all sides. Slowly extending her arms she can feel no earthly boundary as her arms reach into the blackness of space.

As her eyes focus on the magical spectacle of her surrounding, she sees a lone figure hunched down close by. She moves nearer to the figure. As the figure turns to meet her gaze, she recognises the old crone she has seen in her dreams many times before. 'What brings you here Witch?' asks the old reverence. The Witch is for once not sure what to say. The sharpness of her tongue dulled by the spectacle of what her eyes and her mind cannot process.

The Old Crone repeats her question. 'What are you doing here Witch?'

'I am not sure' responds the Witch confused, 'where is this place?'.

The Crone turns her gaze away from the Witch instead reaching to a pool of water at her feet and breaks the surface to create ripples on the black water. The Witch feels the child like need to draw nearer to the motherly Old Crone and drops to her knees beside her at the dark pool edge. 'Where is this place of magic?' she asks again.

'This place, as you call it, is not in your comprehension' answers the Old Crone in a soft tone.

Lifting her withered arm, the Old Crone points to a round portal window in the small room of stars. Instinctively, inquisitively, the Witch stands slowly to her feet and steps up on her toes that she may look through the portal. Outside it is bright as day and she sees a large antler stag grazing in the meadow. There are many people walking slowly with their heads down looking forlorn as they follow a nowhere path walking aimlessly following the path of the stag.

'Who are those people I see?' asks the Witch keeping her gaze fixed on the vision before her.

'Ah, they are those that have lost their way and seek redemption for mistakes made in their lives'.

The Witch can feel their sadness and with a shiver, turns back to the Old Crone.

'You must avoid their fate Witch and not spend your remaining days wishing to be someone else'.

The Witch hears the words of the Old Crone but does not process the meaning. Crouching down again beside the Old Crone, the Witch looks into the ripple pool. The Old Crone reaches again into the pool with her withered hand. Suddenly, withdrawing a small baby squab in the palm of her hand. Offering the small creature, a baby pigeon, towards the Witch.

'Here, take this small creature, it is a symbol of hope and dreams. Your hope and dreams. You must take it inside of you and keep it safe'. Almost instinctively, the Witch takes the small baby bird into her hands. Gently, yet firm enough to contain the struggling creature in the cupped palms of her hands she brings the small bird closer to her face.

'And how exactly will I take this creature inside of me as you ask?' speaks the Witch. Questioning, her eyes lifting again towards the Old Crone.

'You will know' croaks the old woman. 'Come closer and look here into the blackness of the pool that you might find what you seek'.

Still holding the squab, the Witch places her face to the surface of the black water and peers into her own reflection looking back at her. The reflection suddenly reaches up and quickly grabs hold of the Witch pulling her into the pool. There is no time to resist. In an instant, a splash and she is submersed in the black pool. She feels her lungs expand sharply.

Desperately trying to inhale air to breath. Her mouth involuntarily opens to suck in whatever it can and fills quickly with the black that surrounds her. She feels life ebb away. She feels the struggle of life as she gasps to hold onto life itself. In a last moment, she opens her eyes to the watery depth and sees the small squab now limp in her own hand. The Witch opens her mouth wide to gasp what might be her last.

She feels the sudden rush of air as her lungs fill quickly followed by the equally fast exhale that echoes as a scream into the night sky.

Suddenly, her consciousness has returned. The Witch catches back her breath and she finds herself bolt upright in her own bed. Quickly surveying, she recognizes the features of her own bedroom. That familiar ceiling. The dampness of her skin glistens from the moonlight streaming in the bedroom window.

The Witch wipes the sweat from her brow as she wonders the meaning of her strange dream. She feels a tickle in the back of her throat as though something caught. Reaching to her mouth she pulls a small downy feather from the back of her throat and stares with eyes wide at the object. Flashbacks of her meeting with the Old-Crone, and the words spoken, run through her mind. She feels overcome with joy as she realises that all her hopes and dreams for the future are inside of her to find.

Watch with glittering eyes the whole world around you. Because the greatest secrets are hidden in the most unlikely places.

We are frogsnotpigeons. Join us.

BOOKS BY THIS AUTHOR

Natural Frequency

A collection of short stories about an Irish Witch and her companions, a pigeon and a frog. The stories tell of their life challenges through a narrative of dark humor and sarcasm.

Printed in Great Britain
by Amazon